Written by Alcides Villaça
Illustrated by Andrés Sandoval

Translated from the Portuguese by Flávia Rocha,
in collaboration with Endi Bogue Hartigan

First English language edition published in 2020 by Tapioca Stories.
English language edition © 2020 Tapioca Stories
Originally published as O invisível © 2011 Editora 34, Brazil.

Library of Congress Control Number: 2020941178
ISBN: 978-1-7347839-1-9
Printed in China
First Printing, 2020

© 2020 Tapioca Stories
55 Gerard St. #455, Huntington, New York 11743
www.tapiocastories.com

The invisible

Alcides Villaça • Andrés Sandoval

To not be seen at home...
To not be seen at school,
not on the street, not anywhere...

To hear them all talk, invisible.
To peek in the Kitchen, invisible,
To lick from auntie's ice cream...

To make the broom dance
and let the plate drop.

To blow into the cat's face...
To unlace the shoes
of that rascally classmate.

To sing into grandma's ear
the song she loves to hear.

To kiss Mara on the cheek
and poke her brother.
To snatch the pan from the stove,
the sausage from the bun.

To travel far by plane...by boat...
To catch a ride in a hot air balloon...

To sneak into a soccer game
and munch at the candy shop.
To walk into any movie theater.

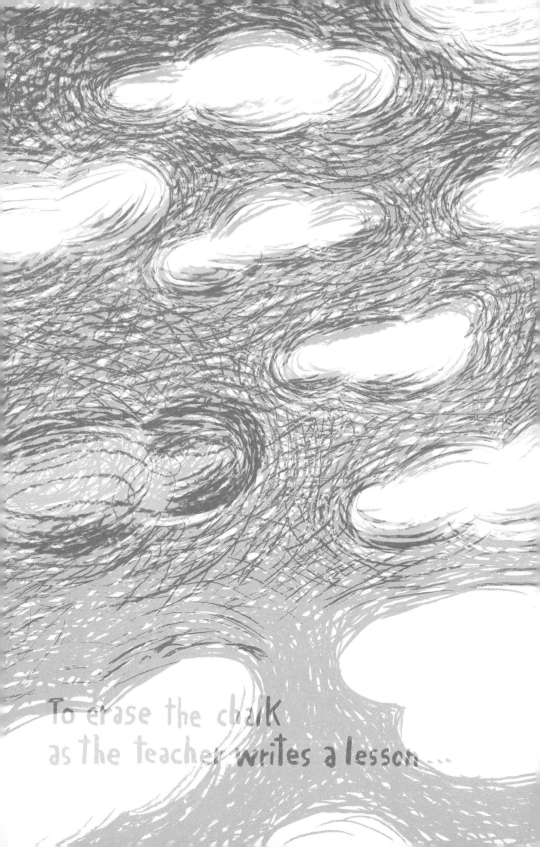

To erase the chalk
as the teacher writes a lesson ...

I can think of so many things,
so many I can't keep count.

So, look, here's something
I'm always wondering:

Do you think that one day
the magic will go away?
Isn't it tiring to be
someone no one can see?

If Someone is never seen,
do they even Know they exist?

Better than being invisible
is to imagine the invisible.

Let them see me.

Let them call me.

Let them find me.

Let Mara give me a kiss
knowing who she kisses.

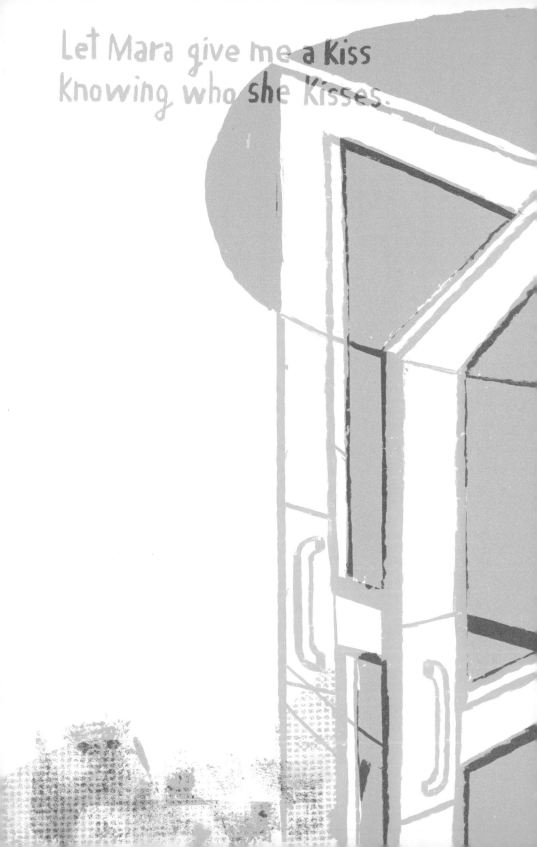